Mindy Kim and the
Yummy Seaweed Business

Don't miss more fun adventures
with **Mindy Kim**!

BOOK 2:
Mindy Kim and the Lunar New Year Parade

Coming soon:

BOOK 3:
Mindy Kim and the Birthday Puppy

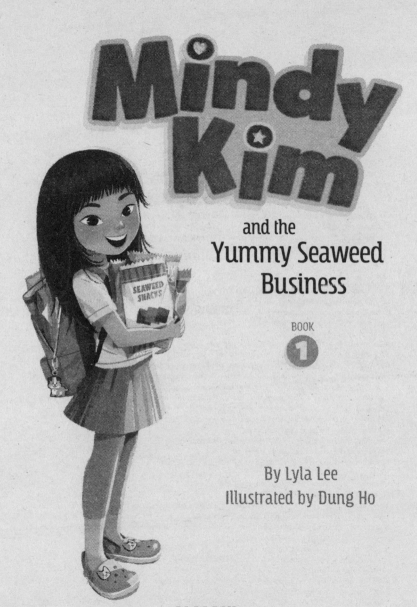

Mindy Kim

and the
Yummy Seaweed Business

BOOK
1

By Lyla Lee
Illustrated by Dung Ho

ALADDIN
New York London Toronto Sydney New Delhi

❤ ALADDIN

An imprint of Simon & Schuster Children's Publishing Division

1230 Avenue of the Americas, New York, New York 10020

First Aladdin paperback edition January 2020

Text copyright © 2020 by Lyla Lee

Illustrations copyright © 2020 by Dung Ho

Also available in an Aladdin hardcover edition.

All rights reserved, including the right of reproduction in whole or in part in any form.

ALADDIN and related logo are registered trademarks of Simon & Schuster, Inc.

For information about special discounts for bulk purchases, please contact Simon & Schuster Special Sales at 1-866-506-1949 or business@simonandschuster.com.

The Simon & Schuster Speakers Bureau can bring authors to your live event. For more information or to book an event contact the Simon & Schuster Speakers Bureau at 1-866-248-3049 or visit our website at www.simonspeakers.com.

Book designed by Laura Lyn DiSiena

The illustrations for this book were rendered digitally.

The text of this book was set in Haboro.

Manufactured in the United States of America 1219 OFF

10 9 8 7 6 5 4 3 2 1

Library of Congress Cataloging-in-Publication Data

Names: Lee, Lyla, author. | Ho, Dung, illustrator.

Title: Mindy Kim and the yummy seaweed business / by Lyla Lee ; illustrated by Dung Ho.

Description: New York : Aladdin, 2020. | Series: Mindy Kim ; 1 | Audience: Ages 6-9 |

Summary: Mindy Kim wants to fit in at her new school, but her favorite lunch leads to scorn, then a thriving business, and finally big trouble.

Identifiers: LCCN 2019026740 (print) | LCCN 2019026741 (eBook) |

ISBN 9781534440074 (paperback) | ISBN 9781534440098 (hardcover) |

ISBN 9781534440081 (eBook)

Subjects: CYAC: Moving, Household–Fiction. | Schools–Fiction. | Korean Americans–Fiction. | Single-parent families–Fiction. | Grief–Fiction.

Classification: LCC PZ7.1.L419 Min 2020 (print) | LCC PZ7.1.L419 (eBook) | DDC [Fic]–dc23

LC record available at https://lccn.loc.gov/2019026740

LC eBook record available at https://lccn.loc.gov/2019026741

For all the new kids out there. You're not alone.

Chapter 1

My name is Mindy Kim.

I'm seven and a half years old. That's old enough to ride a bike around our street, but not old enough to have my own puppy—or at least that's what my dad said.

I don't really agree with him, but our old apartment in California wasn't big enough for a puppy anyway. I looked it up, and the experts on the Internet say that puppies need lots of room to run outdoors.

Now that we've moved into a house with a big backyard, we can really get a puppy! I just have to convince my dad that it's a good idea first.

So far, no such luck. Dad wants me to prove that I can be "responsible" enough for a puppy first . . . and then he'll "consider" getting me one.

I decorated my own room to show Dad I'm "responsible." I'm trying to be more grown-up, so I only put three dog stuffed animals on my bed. There are ten more under my bed, but Dad doesn't need to know that. They'll just have to take turns.

After I finished, I was looking through a website on huskies, one of my *favorite* kinds of dogs, when I heard Dad say, "Mindy? Can you help me with these boxes?"

CRASH!

"Dad!" I ran downstairs to see him standing over a box of broken dishes.

"Oh no!" he said. "These were your mom's favorites."

He looked so sad, like he was about to cry. I wished I'd brought one of my stuffed dogs with me. I'd even let him hug Snowball, my favorite white husky.

I miss Mom, but I know Dad misses her a lot

more. She died a few months ago because she was really sick for a long time.

"It's okay," I said. "It was an accident. Mom wouldn't be mad."

Dad smiled. "No, she wouldn't. She was nice like that."

Dad and I finished unpacking and cleaning up the kitchen. The kitchen in our apartment in California was way smaller, so our things only filled up half the cabinets in our new house.

When we were done, Dad ordered pizza. He remembered to ask for pineapples on top, just the way I like it.

We waited for the pizza in our new dining room. Sitting at the table felt weird. All our stuff looked strange and small in this new, big house.

"Dad?" I asked. "Why did we never live in a house like this in California?"

"Everything is a lot cheaper in Florida than in California," Dad explained. "Plus, I got a big raise for transferring out here."

The pizza finally came. And it smelled so good

that my mouth watered before we even opened the box.

Dad handed me the largest slice.

"So, are you excited for school on Monday?" he asked.

The pizza dropped from my hands and right onto the floor. Oops.

Dad cringed. There was a large greasy, pizza-shaped stain on our new rug. "It's okay, honey. You eat, and I'll clean this up."

But I wasn't hungry anymore. Dad mentioning school had made me lose my appetite. Monday was only two days away. I'd never gone to a new school before. I didn't even know what the kids here would be like! And what if the teachers were mean?

I liked my friends and teachers in California. I wished we could just go back.

Dad returned with some cleaning supplies and frowned when he saw that I wasn't eating any of the pizza.

"Mindy," he said, "this move is going to be better for both of us! We could both use a fresh start."

Then I got a brilliant idea.

"Appa?" I said in my most innocent voice, using the Korean word for "Daddy." "Do you know what would *really* help us have a fresh start?"

Dad shook his head. "I already know what you are going to say. And we can't get a dog right now. You and I have to get settled in first."

Well, dog poop. He read my mind. It was worth a shot.

I was still pouting when Dad picked up the pizza box.

"Do you really not want any of the pizza? I guess I'll just have to finish it all by myself. . . ."

"No!"

I grabbed a slice before Dad could walk away. He smiled and put the pizza back on the table.

"Thanks for the pizza," I said. "But I'm still not looking forward to school."

"I know, sweetie, I know," said Dad. "But can you at least try? Maybe it won't be as bad as you think."

I hoped he was right.

Chapter 2

The more I thought about going to school, the more nervous I was. I couldn't even sleep! By Monday morning I had decided I just wasn't going to go.

"I don't want to go to school!" I yelled, and slammed the door of my room.

"You have to, sweetie," Dad said. "It's the first day! Why don't you give it a chance? You'll be lost if you don't go today!"

I groaned but came back out.

Dad was right. Moving to a new neighborhood on the other side of the country was confusing enough. The last thing I needed was to be even more confused.

"Okay, fine," I said. "But I get to eat ice cream when I come back."

"I'll have a bowl of mint chocolate chip ice cream waiting for you on the dinner table," promised Dad. "With chocolate syrup and sprinkles! Just the way you like it."

I sat in the back seat and didn't say anything the entire way to school.

Dad made funny faces in the mirror.

I didn't smile.

He told a funny joke.

I didn't laugh.

He said, "Look, Mindy! A cute dog!"

It was hard, but I didn't look.

I was too mad at Dad for making me go to a new school. For moving me here. Even though I knew why we moved here, that didn't mean I felt any better about it.

We finally arrived at Wishbone Elementary School. It was pretty for a school, and right by the beach too. But it wasn't enough. It didn't have Diya, one of my best friends. And it didn't have the big hills that we could roll down during recess.

I watched as the other kids got off the school buses. My old school had kids of many different colors. But here, no one looked like me.

I was almost out of the car when Dad said, "Don't forget your lunch!"

The only thing that was the same was my lunch. Dad had packed me the same rice, kimchi, rolled eggs, and dried seaweed snacks that I had eaten for lunch in California.

Lunch was my favorite subject already.

Chapter 3

My new teacher's name is Mrs. Potts. It's easy to remember, because it's just "pots" with another *t*. I asked Dad if I could ask her where the extra *t* came from, but he said it would be rude.

"Welcome!" said Mrs. Potts when I walked into the classroom. "You must be . . . Min-jung." She frowned as she tried to say my Korean name. "Do you have an English name?"

"I go by Mindy," I told her, like Dad told me to do.

"Oh, Mindy! What a pretty name!" Mrs. Potts smiled. "Have a seat wherever you want."

I didn't like Mrs. Potts. I missed Ms. Lin, my old

teacher in California. Ms. Lin said my Korean name was pretty too.

The only empty seat was by a girl with blond pigtails and pink glasses. She was so pretty! It was hard not to stare.

"Hi!" she said when I sat down in my seat. "My name is Sally. What is your name?"

"Mindy," I said. "How old are you?"

"I'm seven. I just had my birthday."

"Nice! I'm seven and a half. My birthday is in February."

"Cool! Are you new?" Sally asked. "Where are you from?"

"I'm from California," I said.

"Wow, that's really far away!"

I wanted to talk more with Sally, but then class started. Mrs. Potts told us the classroom rules. There were too many rules to remember.

Soon, it was lunchtime. I wanted to sit with Sally, but her table was full, so I had to go sit somewhere else. I found a table that had a few extra seats and sat at the very edge.

Back at my old school, I always sat with Diya and Izzy, my two best friends. With them by my side, I never felt lonely. But now, with no one to call my friend, I felt really alone, like the lost penguin in a nature show I had watched with Dad. The little penguin was all alone, a black speck on the white ice, with its friends and family miles and miles away. I cried when I watched that episode, and I kind of felt like crying now.

I took out my lunch box, which had a golden retriever puppy on it. It always made me happy, because the puppy looked like it was smiling.

Well, I thought. *At least my lunch box is cute.*

I opened it and took out my seaweed, kimchi, rolled eggs, and rice.

"What is that?" asked a girl at my table. She pointed at my dried seaweed packs.

"Dried seaweed!" I said. "It's yummy."

"And that?" She pointed at my kimchi.

I blinked at her. How could she not know what kimchi was?

"It's kimchi," I explained. "It's spicy cabbage."

She wrinkled her nose. "It smells."

"Wait," said a boy sitting next to her. "Did she just say that she was eating *seaweed*? Like, from the ocean?"

He laughed, and a few of his friends joined in too. By then *everyone* at the table was staring at me. My cheeks turned bright red.

Suddenly, I wasn't hungry anymore. I wanted to run far, far away. Or go hide in the bathroom somewhere. But we had to go back to class soon, so it wasn't really worth the trouble.

From across the room, Sally frowned at me but didn't say anything.

I thought at least recess would be fun, but being the new kid was boring. Everyone else, including Sally, already had friends to play with. I ended up sitting on the swings by myself. I have always loved swinging, kicking my legs super fast to see if I can go over the top of the swings. But it's not as fun if you're swinging alone.

I hated being the new kid.

Chapter 4

Finally, my very first day ended. Eunice-unni came to pick me up after school. Dad usually works late, so he hired her as my babysitter. *Unni* means "big sister" in Korean. She's not really my sister, but I have to call her that to be polite. Yeah, it's pretty confusing for me, too.

Eunice-unni is in high school. Dad and I met her over the weekend so we could make sure she was okay. I asked her the important questions like, "Do you think puppies are cute?" and "What is your favorite type of ice cream?"

She agreed that puppies are cute but then said that her favorite ice cream flavor is vanilla.

One out of two is better than nothing, I guess.

Eunice-unni said I could meet her dog when she picked me up from school. I ran when I saw her car in the parking lot. It was easy to find because it was blue.

"I like your car," I said. "Blue is my favorite color."

"It's mine, too!"

That was almost enough to make up for the fact that her favorite ice cream flavor was vanilla. Almost.

"Can I really meet your dog today?"

"Yes!" Eunice-unni beamed so I could see her braces. "You can play with him at my house. He's a little Maltese named Oliver. I'm so excited for you to meet him!"

I was excited to meet Oliver too! I'd only seen pictures of Maltese dogs, and they looked so fluffy! I bounced up and down in my seat.

Eunice-unni drove us to her house. Her mom was there and so was Oliver!

Oliver jumped up and down when I walked into the house. I got down to my knees, and he started licking my face. He was so cute and looked like a soft

little cloud. I wished I had a dog like him. "Maltese" was now officially on the list of my favorite dog breeds.

Mrs. Park, Eunice-unni's mom, came over to say hi. She was wearing plastic gloves covered with red pepper paste. I could tell by the smell coming from the kitchen that she was making kimchi.

"Hi, Mindy, it's so nice to meet you!" said Mrs. Park. "I've heard so many things about you!"

I hate when grown-ups say that. You never know if they've heard good things or bad things. I smiled big and wide, just in case.

"How was school?" Mrs. Park asked.

"School was okay," I said.

I didn't tell them about what happened at lunch. I was still too embarrassed.

"Can I go play with Oliver until my dad comes?" I asked Eunice-unni before Mrs. Park could ask me any more questions.

"Sure! His box of toys is in the living room."

I ran to the living room, with Oliver following close behind. My day was better already.

How could I be sad with a cute dog nearby?

Chapter 5

The next morning, Dad packed me the same thing for lunch: rice, dried seaweed, kimchi, and rolled eggs. I meant to tell him that I wanted something different, but we didn't have time. Our toaster had caught on fire, so Dad was already late for work.

"I didn't know you were supposed to clean the toaster," Dad said as he drove me to school. "Your mom must have always taken care of it before she got sick."

I didn't know that either, but I was surprised Dad didn't. Dad is a grown-up. Aren't grown-ups supposed to know everything?

The second day of school was less scary than

the first. But I was still nervous about lunch. What if everyone laughed at me again?

I decided to be a little brave and make goals. Dad says he always has to "make goals" at his job. Things that you want to happen. Goals sounded like something adults made, but I was trying to be more grown-up now.

At my desk, I flipped over to a new page in my Shiba Inu notebook and wrote down my goals in sparkly blue ink.

1. Don't get laughed at during lunch again.
2. Try to make a new friend.
3. Convince Dad that a puppy would be the best idea ever.

It wasn't going to be easy, but I did feel kind of better after writing everything down.

Class passed by really quickly, and soon it was time for lunch. Before Sally left, I took a deep breath and said, "Hey, Sally. Can I sit with you at your lunch table?"

I was scared that she'd say no, but I reminded myself to be a little brave.

Sally looked surprised but smiled. "Okay, sure!"

Phew! I smiled back. That wasn't so bad! And now I had someone who actually wanted to eat lunch with me!

Sally and I walked to her table. But instead of feeling glad that I was sitting with Sally, I still felt super nervous. What if Sally and her friends made fun of my food too?

I slowly opened my lunch box and all my containers. Everyone at the table stared, just like they did yesterday.

I was prepared to be laughed at again when Sally held out her hand. "Can I try some of the seaweed?"

"What?" I asked, surprised.

Sally shrugged. "My mom always says I should try things out before I decide I don't like them."

I handed her the packet of seaweed. It was the spicy kind that you can eat as a snack without rice.

She opened the packet and put a little piece of seaweed in her mouth.

She chewed, her eyes wide.

I was worried that she didn't like it, but then she exclaimed, "Hey! This is really good!"

Everyone looked at Sally. Then, a boy from our class—Charlie, I think— asked, "Can I try too?"

"Sure!"

Charlie ate the seaweed. But the moment it touched his mouth, he spat it back out. "Ew! It feels so weird! Like paper!"

Sally rolled her eyes. "You didn't even eat it!"

"Let me try!" another boy said.

"You better actually eat it, Dill," said Sally. "Don't spit it out like Charlie."

"I won't!"

Sally nodded at me, and I handed Dill a piece of seaweed.

Unlike Charlie, Dill kept the seaweed in his mouth and chewed. "Wow, this is actually good!"

"Well, of course it's good!" I replied. "If you didn't know what dried seaweed was for all this time, you've been missing out!"

Soon everyone at my table was asking to try the dried seaweed. Before I knew it, I didn't have any left for myself.

I ate the rest of my lunch, but it wasn't the same. I was happy that no one had teased me today, but I was sad I didn't have any seaweed left for me. My plan had worked well—too well!

"Sorry everyone ate your seaweed," said Sally. "You should have asked us to trade something with you!"

"I can do that?" I asked.

"Sure, why not? You gave us something. Shouldn't you get something in return? It's only fair."

She had a point. I looked around. Everyone else was still enjoying their lunches. They all had cool snacks too, like Oreos, Pringles, Nutella bites, and fruit snacks. We always just got Korean snacks, because Dad only had time to go shopping at the Korean market. I love Korean snacks, but eating the same snacks over and over again gets kind of boring.

My mouth watered. I was surrounded by these yummy snacks, and all I had for lunch was boring white rice and side dishes. And I still didn't have any friends except maybe Sally.

I kept on thinking as I ate the rest of my sad lunch.

Suddenly, I had a brilliant plan. A very yummy seaweed business plan!

Chapter 6

When Dad picked me up from Eunice-unni's house later that evening, I asked, "Can we stop by the Korean market?"

Dad frowned. "What do you need to buy? We already have a lot of food at home."

"It's for school," I said. "It's important!"

Dad looked confused, but he drove to the Korean market without any more questions. There aren't a lot of Asian markets in Florida, and the closest Korean one is an hour away, in Orlando. And that meant we were super close to Disney World!

When he told me that we were going to move to

Florida, Dad promised to take me to Disney World. I reminded him of the promise.

"I'll take you there when things are less busy at work, sweetie," he said.

I knew it meant that we'd probably never go. It made me sad, but it's not Dad's fault. He's always busy, and he worked really hard when we were back in California too. I just wish his boss gave him more breaks.

The Korean market in Orlando isn't as big as the one in California. It's also really old. But it still has all my favorite snacks, like Pepero chocolate sticks, Choco Pie, and shrimp crackers. So it's okay in my book.

Today, though, I didn't go for any of those snacks. I was on a mission. It was time to put part one of Operation Yummy Seaweed Business in motion!

I ran right for the dried seaweed aisle. Since people like to eat seaweed with all sorts of stuff, there are lots of different kinds of seaweed on the shelves: dried seaweed that you put in soup, salted seaweed that you eat with rice, and large, plain seaweed sheets that you use to wrap kimbap and sushi.

I grabbed a bunch of spicy seaweed snacks and put them in our shopping basket.

Dad raised his eyebrows. "This is for school?" he asked.

I gave him a firm nod. He still looked suspicious but didn't make me put any back.

I dropped a few more packs of different-flavored seaweed snacks into the basket too.

Dad shot me another weird look. "Okay, Mindy, I think you have enough to last you until winter break."

I gave Dad a big smile but didn't say anything.

After a few more minutes of wandering the store, Dad yawned. "Ready to go, kiddo?"

I grabbed his hand and gave him my best smile.

"Yes. Thanks, Appa," I said.

He hugged me. "Sure."

I glanced back toward the snacks. "Wait, can we get some Choco Pies before we leave?"

SEAWEED
해조류
Crunch
$2.00
SEAWEED SNACK
Seaweed Snack
$2.95
$2.95
CRISPY
SEAWE
ROASTED Seaweed Snack
Organic
Seaweed Snack

Dad grinned, like he knew I was going to ask him that. He always knows everything.

He ruffled my hair. "Why not? We need to celebrate your first few days of school anyway."

When we got home, we ate our Choco Pies. That night I dreamed of pies, California, and seaweed, and hoped my third day of school would go just how I wanted.

Chapter 7

On Wednesday morning, I told Dad to put ten packs of the seaweed into my lunch box.

"Ten? You will never eat all of those in one day, Mindy," Dad said.

"It's an experiment!" I replied. "Plus, I want to share with some of the kids in my class."

It wasn't a complete lie. Dad sighed, but he stuffed all ten packs of seaweed into my lunch box. Along with the rice and side dishes, my lunch box looked extra full. I was afraid that it might explode and seaweed would fly out everywhere. But it didn't.

At school, I sat next to Sally again. She had blue ribbons in her hair today, and they reminded me of the ocean. Mom, Dad, and I loved to go to the beach in California. Even though there was one right by my new school, I didn't know when I'd be able to go with Dad.

At lunch, Dill asked, "Do you have any more of that dried seaweed?"

Sally shot me a look, and I crossed my arms. It was my chance!

"Yeah, but you have to trade me something for it!" I said.

He shrugged. "Okay. I have gummy worms. Do you want some?"

He held up a small baggie of sour gummy worms. They were green apple-flavored. My favorite!

"Sure! Let's shake on it."

I held out my hand, like I had seen people do on TV. He shook my hand, and then we swapped snacks.

"Hey," said a girl with red hair. Her nose was wrinkled, but she held out a bag of Cheetos. "I want to try the seaweed everyone is talking about. Want to trade?"

"Sure! What's your name?"

"Amanda."

"Hi, I'm Mindy!"

I shook hands with her, too.

Soon a whole line of people had formed to trade snacks with me. I wasn't sure if I had enough!

"Wow!" Sally said. "It looks like business is booming!"

She said it kind of funny, like she was just repeating something she'd heard on TV.

"Yup, and it's all thanks to you! Thanks for the idea."

"No problem."

She gave me a big grin.

"Hey," I said. "Do you want some of the snacks everyone gave me? I can't eat this all by myself!"

"Sure, thanks!"

I gave Sally half of my pile of snacks. She grinned, and we happily munched on everything for the rest of lunch.

The plan was working!

Chapter 8

The next day, a line of kids formed in the cafeteria even before I got out my packs of seaweed.

"Okay," I said. "Everyone, show me your snacks!"

I examined the snacks to see which ones were the best. Everyone had pretty good snacks, except the kids with vegetable sticks and vanilla cake. Dad always makes me eat vegetables at home, so there was no way I was going to eat them at school. And vanilla is just gross. Plain and simple.

When I skipped over the boy with the vanilla cake, he said, "Hey! How come everyone else gets to trade with you except me?"

"I don't like vanilla, sorry," I said. I wasn't really

sorry, but Dad always says it's polite to apologize when someone is upset. And this boy looked *really* mad! His face was turning red like a tomato. He looked like he was going to cry.

I almost told him that he could get the seaweed packs himself at the Korean market. But I didn't. Because then everyone would hear, and no one would need me to trade snacks with them anymore. I'd have no friends left.

I decided to ignore him. Maybe he'd just go back to his seat.

But instead of leaving, the boy stood there, staring angrily at me and the other kids as I traded snacks with them.

Sally came over to sit next to me.

"That's Brandon," she whispered. "Don't worry about him. He's a big baby. No one really likes him."

She glared at Brandon until he finally walked back to his table.

"Thanks," I said.

"No problem!"

At recess, Sally and I were on the swings together when she asked, "Did you ever think about *selling* the seaweed snacks?"

I almost fell off my swing. "Huh?"

"I mean, think about it! Everyone loves the snacks a *lot*. And getting snacks back for them is good, but then you have to eat everything and it's too much food. What if you ask for money instead?"

"But what would I do with the money? I don't need to buy anything."

Sally shrugged. "It was just a suggestion. My mom says you have to take advantage of every good business opportunity. She works for a really big company and is always saying that."

"Wow, that's so cool!"

Sally talking about her mom made me miss my mom. I wished my mom were here to give me good advice too.

I got off my swing. There were only a few minutes left of recess.

"Tag, you're it!" I tapped Sally on the shoulder before breaking into a run.

"Hey, I wasn't ready!" Sally protested, but she jumped off her swing and started chasing me anyway.

She caught me right away, but I wasn't mad.

Did I finally have my first real friend at school?

Chapter 9

Dad was working late today, so Eunice-unni came over to our house to stay with me. The house was big and scary without Dad, but Eunice-unni brought Oliver the Maltese with her, so it was okay!

I played fetch with Oliver while Eunice unni finished her homework. Oliver was so fluffy that whenever he ran, he looked like a bouncing cloud. He was *so* cute.

Seeing Oliver run around our house made me want a dog even more. Playing with him made me so happy!

"Hey, Mindy," said Eunice-unni. "I'm done with

my homework. Wanna walk Oliver around the block with me?"

"Sure!"

Eunice-unni let me hold Oliver's leash as we walked around my neighborhood. Compared to my old neighborhood, everything was so *green*. There were palm trees and bushes everywhere, like in a jungle. My neighbors all had really big yards with tall grass. Back in California, it didn't rain much, so everything was brown. Florida seemed like a whole different planet!

Oliver got really muddy from wandering outside. Eunice-unni said it was okay, since we could just wash him in the bathtub.

"He needed a bath anyway," she said with a smile.

Dad didn't get home until really late. By the time the garage door opened, Eunice-unni and I had already finished bathing Oliver and eaten dinner.

When he got home, Dad was so tired that he fell asleep on the couch!

I nudged him softly on the shoulder.

"Appa," I said. "Shouldn't you sleep in your bed?"

Dad startled awake, but then relaxed when he saw me.

"Oh, hi, Mindy," he said, rubbing his eyes. "Yeah, I really should. What time is it?"

"It's ten. Can you tuck me into bed?"

"Oh wow. And I haven't eaten dinner yet."

I gasped. "You didn't eat dinner at work?"

"No, I didn't have time. It's fine. I'll grab something later. Come on, sweetie. Let's go."

Dad tucked me in, but I couldn't sleep because I was too worried. Dad was so tired! And he forgot to eat dinner! What if he got sick like Mom?

I decided to take matters into my own hands. I'm not sure exactly what that means, but I've heard Dad say it before. I think it means doing things yourself.

After Dad finished eating and went to his room, I got out of bed and tiptoed to the kitchen. I'm not allowed to touch the stove yet, but Dad says I can use the electric kettle to boil water since all you have to do is press the switch. I put water in the kettle and turned it on.

As the water started to boil, I got on my step

stool so I could reach the tea. Dad bought a cute pink step stool with white hearts just for me! With the stool, I could reach for a chamomile tea bag with no problem. Dad likes to drink chamomile tea because he says it helps him relax. I couldn't wait to surprise him with the tea!

I carefully carried the mug of tea to Dad's room. I was about to open the bedroom door when I heard sniffling noises. Dad was crying!

"Appa!"

With one hand still clutching the mug, I flung open the door.

"Mindy!" Dad bolted up from the bed, like I'd caught him doing something wrong. He looked really embarrassed!

But he was also definitely crying. Ever since Mom died, Dad cries all the time.

"I made you some tea so you could feel better!" I held out the cup of tea.

Dad smiled, but he still looked sad. "Thank you, Mindy. That's really sweet of you. Now please go back to bed. It's way past your bedtime."

"Okay. Good night, Dad."

"Good night." He took a sip of the tea and waved.

I went back to my room. But even when I was in my bed, I kept thinking about how sad Dad looked. And then I thought about how I always felt better whenever I played with Oliver.

I wanted to cheer up Dad, but I couldn't do it alone. Maybe Sally was right. Maybe I could sell my seaweed snacks for money. Then, I could buy a puppy for Dad and me! Since it's impossible to be sad with a cute puppy around, Dad wouldn't be so sad and lonely, and I could have the dog I'd always wanted. It'd be like hitting two birds with one stone!

I snuck downstairs, got Dad's tablet, and brought it back to my room. Puppies are expensive if you buy them from breeders, but not if you adopt them from a shelter!

On the Internet, I found a nearby shelter and scrolled through the available dogs. They were all so cute that I couldn't choose! But they also looked so sad, kind of like Dad.

Don't worry! I thought while scrolling through

the dog pictures. *I'll adopt one of you guys soon! Then you and Dad can both be happy.*

After a while, I started getting sleepy. I set Dad's tablet down next to me on the bed and fell asleep, dreaming of cute puppies and Dad's smiling face.

Chapter 10

On Friday, Dad didn't say anything when I packed dozens of seaweed snacks into my bag. He didn't say anything at all. I think he was too tired. And sad.

Don't worry, Dad! I thought. *I'll get us a puppy real soon!*

During quiet reading time, I went to the back of the classroom. Mrs. Potts looked up from where she was grading worksheets.

"Mindy?" she said with a frown. "Is everything all right?"

"Yup!" I gave her a big smile. "I finished my book, so I just wanted to get markers and paper so I could draw, if that's okay!"

"Well, all right."

She went back to her work, and I got out my box of markers and a piece of paper from my desk.

"I'm gonna do it!" I whispered to Sally. "Operation Yummy Seaweed Business is a go!"

Sally whispered back, "That's great! What are the markers and paper for?"

"You'll see!"

On the paper, I wrote in big letters: SEAWEED SNACKS FOR SALE. ONLY $1 EACH!

I put a smiley face at the bottom of the paper as a finishing touch.

"Nice!" Sally said. "It'll get people's attention for sure!"

When it was lunchtime, I opened my lunch box to show everyone my seaweed snacks. Beside me, Sally held up the sign I made.

"Attention!" I said to the table. "From now on, you can get a seaweed snack for only one dollar each! This is a good deal! Candy from the cafeteria costs *at least* two dollars."

Everyone seemed to think a dollar was a good

price. At least, no one complained. Like they had the day before, everyone lined up for a seaweed snack. I didn't have anywhere to put the dollar bills, so I ended up putting all of them in my lunch box.

And Sally was right: business was booming!

Lunch was almost over when Brandon came over to my table. He grinned at me, but not in a nice way.

"You know it's against the rules to sell things at school, right?"

I looked at Sally with wide eyes. She stared back at me. I don't think she knew that rule either.

"You're making it up!" Sally said, crossing her arms in front of her chest.

Brandon stuck his nose in the air. "No, I'm not. I'm telling on you two."

He glanced around from left to right. I didn't have to be a mind reader to know that he was looking for a teacher. Brandon broke into a run.

"Stop him!" I yelled at Sally.

Sally chased after Brandon. I wanted to chase

Brandon right away too, but I had to make sure the money was safely in my lunch box first.

We ran as fast as we could across the cafeteria. But it was too late. Before Sally or I could catch him, Brandon ran to Mrs. Potts, who was on lunch duty today.

Brandon took a big breath.

"No!" Sally and I both screamed.

Mrs. Potts looked at us, confused. "Is everything all right, girls?"

Brandon yelled, "Mrs. Potts! Mindy is selling her seaweed snacks! That's against the rules!"

Everyone sitting at the tables around us froze. I gulped. Sally looked pretty scared too.

Mrs. Potts looked more confused than angry. "Selling her . . . seaweed snacks? What do you mean, Brandon?"

"Mindy is selling her weird seaweed snacks for money," whined Brandon. "She has dollar bills crammed in her lunch box."

Mrs. Potts turned to look at me. "Is this true, Mindy?"

I stared down at my feet. My lips started trembling. All I wanted was to make Dad happy. I didn't know selling my snacks would get me in trouble.

"Mindy?" Mrs. Potts tried again. "Can you please look up at me?"

I did. Mrs. Potts was frowning at me like she had on the first day of school, when she couldn't say my Korean name. Everyone else was staring at me too. Even Sally.

Suddenly, I was really mad. Why was I the only one getting in trouble, when asking for money wasn't even *my* idea in the first place?

I pointed at Sally. "It was *her* idea!" I blurted. "I was trading snacks when Sally told me I should ask for money. I didn't even know it was against the rules! No one told me. I just moved here!"

It worked. Mrs. Potts looked at Sally, surprised. "Sally? Is this true?"

Sally's mouth dropped open. Her eyes got really shiny all of a sudden, like she was about to cry. I felt really bad.

"I never *told* you that you should!" Sally yelled

at me. "I only suggested it. You didn't *have* to ask for money."

"You two are both bad!" Brandon interrupted. "You need to get kicked out of school!"

"What are you even talking about?" Sally yelled at him. "Shut up!"

"Yeah, Brandon. Be quiet! Why would we get kicked out of school?"

"Everyone, please!" Mrs. Potts yelled, stopping all of us.

By then, a big crowd had formed around us to see all the action.

"Take deep breaths to calm down. Brandon, no one is getting kicked out of school, and you are in trouble too, for running around the cafeteria and causing a commotion."

I cheered on the inside.

"All three of you, walk down to the principal's office right now. I'll have to call your parents."

"What?" Sally yelled. "Thanks a lot, Mindy."

"Why are you blaming me for *your* idea?"

"Miss Johnson! Miss Kim! Please go to the principal's office at once!"

Oh boy. Mrs. Potts used the last name card. I was *really* in trouble now.

I sighed and walked out of the cafeteria with Sally and Brandon.

Chapter 11

Even before he spoke, I knew that our principal was gonna be really mean and scary, and not just because his name is Dr. Mortimer. He is really skinny and tall, and behind his square glasses, he has big, bulging eyes like a bat. Only, bats are pretty cute once you get over the fact that they look like little aliens. Dr. Mortimer isn't cute at all.

He looked up from his computer when I came in. I really wished the secretary had let me come in with Sally or even with Brandon—*that* was how much I didn't want to be in Dr. Mortimer's office alone. I'd figured we would all be getting in trouble together. But no such luck. She'd said the principal would see us one by one.

"Min-jung Kim?" he asked, peering down at me over his narrow glasses. His voice was all gravelly, like it belonged to a monster in a scary movie. I'm not supposed to watch scary movies, but once, I snuck downstairs to watch one while Dad was asleep. Afterward, I was so scared that I had to sleep with my night-light on for two whole months.

"That's me," I said, sitting in front of his desk. "But I go by Mindy."

"Mindy . . . ," he said. But unlike Mrs. Potts, Dr. Mortimer didn't seem happy with my nickname. "So, Mrs. Potts told me that you were selling snacks on school property. Is that true?"

Dad always said it was good to be honest, so I replied, "Yes, but I didn't know it was against the school rules. I just moved here this week!"

"I see." Dr. Mortimer frowned. He looked at his computer screen again. "And what is this about . . . seaweed?"

He sounded really confused.

"My dad always packs me seaweed snacks from the Korean market. Everyone really liked them, so I traded with everybody for their snacks before I started asking for money."

"Seaweed snacks?" He wrinkled his nose.

"They're yummy! I have some if you want to try—"

"That won't be necessary," Dr. Mortimer said, cutting me off.

He looked at me like my grandma looks at flies while trying to catch them with a swatter. "Selling snacks is strictly forbidden on school grounds. I will let you off with a warning this time because you are new, but please familiarize yourself with the school rules during the weekend before returning to school on Monday. They're online, so you can get your parents to show them to you. Please return to class, Miss Kim. I will e-mail your teacher to let her know my decision."

I didn't even get the chance to tell Dr. Mortimer that I only have one parent, not two. He turned back toward his computer right away. The conversation was over. And so was my seaweed business.

Chapter 12

For the rest of the day, Sally ignored me. She didn't look at me one bit, even though our seats were right next to each other.

Mrs. Potts called all our parents, and I heard someone say that Sally cried in the bathroom while Mrs. Potts called her mom. Mrs. Potts also tried calling my dad, but she had to leave a message. I hoped Dad would forget to call her back.

Even though Sally *had* been the one to tell me that I could sell my seaweed snacks, I still felt kind of bad about getting her into trouble too. She was the first and only friend I'd made here at Wishbone Elementary, but I wasn't sure if we were friends anymore. I'd have no one to play with on the playground again.

Back at home, Dad asked, "How was school today?"

Eunice-unni's mom had given us kimchi dumplings when Dad picked me up, and he was heating them in a pan on the stove as he talked to me. Even though I like dumplings, I wasn't sure if Dad was cooking them right. There was too much hot oil splattering loudly everywhere, the drops all dancing in the pan a little too fast.

"It was . . . okay," I said.

"Just okay?"

Dad's voice sounded weird, a little higher than usual. I hoped against hope that he hadn't heard Mrs. Potts's message.

CRACKLE-CRACKLE-POP! Suddenly, some of the oil splattered out of the pan and onto Dad.

"Ouch!" He jumped back.

"Appa!" I yelled. "Are you okay?"

When Dad turned to look at me, there were tears in his eyes, but he was still smiling. He does that a lot. I think it's because he doesn't want me to worry.

"I'm fine, sweetie. Nothing that good ol' cold water won't fix."

He turned off the stove and turned on the kitchen sink so he could stick his hand into the water.

Then, Dad cleared his throat and asked, "So, what's this about the principal's office? I got a call from Mrs. Potts earlier, but I was waiting for you to bring it up first."

There it was. I sighed.

"I was trading snacks with the other kids," I began. The more I talked, the more my words came tumbling out in a rush. "But then my friend Sally and I got the idea to sell the snacks for money. I didn't know selling snacks was against the rules, but it is, and someone told on us. So we got sent to the principal's office."

"Selling snacks? What snacks?" Dad looked really confused.

"Seaweed snacks," I said.

"Oh. So *that's* why you needed to pack so many seaweed snacks. You know, you can always ask me if you need something, Mindy. I don't understand why you felt the need to sell snacks to raise money. I hope you returned all the money you got from the kids. What did you even need the money for?"

"Mrs. Potts and the other teachers returned the money to everyone," I said. "And . . . I wanted it to be a surprise."

Dad frowned. "A surprise?"

I nodded sadly. "I know you're still sad because Mom died, so I wanted to cheer you up by buying you a puppy. Because puppies make me happy, and I want you to be happy too."

Suddenly, Dad looked like he was about to cry again. "Oh, Mindy. You didn't have to do that."

He pulled me into a big hug.

There were some sniffly sounds, but when Dad finally pulled away, he quickly wiped away his tears. He looked really embarrassed.

"You don't have to be embarrassed, Dad. You can cry. Everyone gets sad sometimes."

Mom used to always tell me that when I cried. Dad must have recognized the words, because his eyes started watering again.

"I know, Mindy. But I can't help but think that this wouldn't have happened if I were a little better at being a dad. I'm so sorry, Mindy."

"No!" I yelled. "You are the best dad. You do everything you can to make me happy. You're just really busy, that's all."

Dad sighed. "I know. I have to fix that."

After he finished making the dumplings, Dad asked, "So . . . why did you feel the need to trade snacks in the first place? Mindy, if you're not happy with the snacks I pack you, you can always tell me."

I shook my head. "It wasn't because of the snacks. Well, okay. At first, it was because everyone else had really cool snacks. But then, I did it to make friends. Everyone liked me when I gave them seaweed snacks. They talked to me too."

"Aw, you don't need snacks to make people like you, Mindy! I'm sure people will love you just the way you are, like they did in California."

I shook my head again. "No, they won't. It's not the same. I'm the only Asian girl in the entire school! Everyone made fun of me on the first day. Now, some kids still look at me kind of funny, but they all talked to me when we traded snacks."

"I'm sorry, sweetie. The snack thing was a good idea, but try to find another way to make friends, okay? One that won't get you into trouble. I know it's hard, but I have complete faith in you, Mindy. You're a smart girl, and I'm sure you'll figure something out."

I sighed.

"Okay," I said, even though I had no idea how I was gonna make new friends. "I'll try."

Chapter 13

On Monday morning, I didn't want to go to school. I didn't even want to get out of bed!

I pulled my blanket over my head. Maybe if I hid well enough, Dad would forget I was here and leave the house without me.

I'd promised Dad that I would try to make new friends again, but I was still scared. Without my snack-trading business, no one would want to talk to me. Sally was still mad at me. And I didn't want to be alone.

Soft footsteps came from the staircase. Then, Dad was there, sitting on the edge of my bed. He gently pulled the covers down, and I gave him my best sad-puppy-dog face.

"Appa, do I *have* to go to school?"

He smiled. "Yup, it's a Monday. That means school for you and work for me. Mindy, why don't you ask a friend if she

wants to come over during the weekend? That way you'll have something to look forward to and the week will fly right by."

I sighed. "But I don't have anyone to play with."

Dad frowned. "Didn't you say you had a friend from school? Her name was Sally, right?"

I picked at my blanket. "Sally isn't my friend anymore. We had a fight because she was the one who said I should sell seaweed snacks in the first place."

Dad frowned. "Oh, Mindy. I'm sure she only meant to help. Why don't you apologize and invite her over to our house?"

I pulled the covers over my head again. "What if she says no?"

Instead of answering, Dad slowly placed his hands on my sides and started wiggling his fingers up and down. He was tickling me!

"Ah!" I yelled, bursting out of my blankets. "That tickles!"

Dad let go, and I leaped out of bed.

"Always works like a charm." Dad chuckled.

"Come on, Mindy. You're going to be late for school, and I'm going to be late for work."

I didn't care about being late for school. But I didn't want Dad to be late for work.

"Okay," I said sadly.

To make myself feel better, I dragged myself out of bed and went to my closet. I picked out a corgi T-shirt and bright pink pants. Cute clothes always make me feel a tiny bit better, even on days I feel gloomy.

Dad smiled when he saw my outfit.

"Very cute! Let's go."

I put on my pink Crocs and got into the car.

Chapter 14

Mrs. Potts announced that the whole class was banned from trading snacks. "Banned," she explained, meant that we weren't allowed to do something. Trading snacks technically wasn't against school rules, but she didn't want us to get any other ideas.

Everyone looked disappointed, but no one looked as disappointed as I was.

Now that we weren't allowed to trade snacks anymore, no one even glanced my way. Sally was still ignoring me. It was like I was a ghost.

I was kind of mad at Sally. If it weren't for her, I'd have been able to keep my snack trading ring and would still have friends. Why was *she* still mad at me for something *she* did?

But then I thought about what Dad had said about Sally just trying to help. That was probably true. She *was* trying to be helpful.

When it was time for lunch, Sally left the classroom without me, so I ate alone. It made me so sad that I made up my mind. I was going to say sorry to Sally during recess. Or try to, anyway.

When the bell rang for recess, I slowly walked outside. There was no point in running to the playground like everyone else. I had no one to play with. It was really sunny, and there wasn't a cloud in the sky. I could hear seagulls crying above my head.

I stared up at the seagulls. If only the birds could be my friends.

When I got to the swings, I saw Sally playing with a few other girls. The girls waved at me, but Sally turned her head and pretended not to see me.

I looked down at my Crocs. They're pink and have little Shiba Inu puppy pins on them. The Crocs are my favorite pair of shoes, since they're the last shoes Mom bought for me.

Mom always said I should try my best to be nice to other kids. And so did Dad.

I decided I needed to try my best right then and there. I scrunched up my hands into fists and said in a loud voice, "Sally, I'm sorry!"

Everyone went quiet. I looked up to see that everyone around us was staring at Sally and me. But I didn't care. I was here on a mission.

Sally still had her back turned toward me. Her shoulders were tensed up, so I knew she wasn't ready to forgive me yet. But at least she was listening.

I continued, "I know you were just trying to help when you said I should sell my seaweed snacks. You're right. I didn't *have* to follow your suggestion. I'm sorry I got you into trouble too. Can we still be friends?"

Sally slowly turned around. She didn't look like she completely forgave me, but it was a start.

"Thanks for saying sorry. My mom was mad at me, and I got yelled at a lot."

I felt bad. I wished there were a way to make it up to Sally.

"I'm really sorry," I said. "Do you want me to push you on the swings? I'll push you if you push me next."

She shrugged. "Okay."

I ran to the swings. Sally sat down, and I pushed her so she went flying into the air.

"WHEE!" she yelled.

She looked happy, and I was happy that she was happy. Her ponytail bounced up and down as she rode the swings.

Then, it was my turn. Sally got off, and I sat down. The seat was warm from Sally's butt.

Sally pushed me so I went up, up into the sky. From way up high, I could see the ocean! The water was blue and super pretty, and so was the white sand on the beach next to our school. I wished we were allowed to go there during recess.

Too soon, we had to go back to class. And for the first time, I was sad to leave the playground.

Chapter 15

During our class visit to the school library, I was reading a book about sleepovers when I remembered what Dad had said about inviting Sally over. Hopefully, a sleepover could help patch things up between Sally and me for good.

"Hey," I whispered to Sally. "Wanna sleep over at my house on Friday? We have lots of good snacks, not just seaweed! You can have all the snacks you want."

I was afraid she'd say no, but Sally said, "Sounds fun! I'll ask my mom, and she'll call your mom. What's your number?"

I froze, like I always do when someone mentions Mom.

Sally looked worried. "What's wrong?"

I didn't want Sally to know I didn't have a mom. Not yet. Back in my old school, kids always looked at me funny after they found out what happened to my mom.

"I live with my dad," I finally said. "She can call him!"

Sally shrugged. "Okay!"

And I was pretty happy for the rest of the day. Even though I didn't have my seaweed business, maybe my plan had worked a little after all. I actually felt like I had a new friend. Maybe this school wouldn't be as bad as I thought.

After school, Eunice-unni and I drove back to my house. Dad said he was working late today again, so we were prepared with a whole list of games.

But when we got home, I saw Dad's car parked in the driveway.

"That's weird," said Eunice-unni. "Did I miss a text from him or something? I could have sworn he said he was gonna be late today."

She walked me to the door and rang the bell. Dad opened the door, grinning wide.

"Hi, Eunice. Sorry I didn't give you the heads-up. I was able to reschedule some things today, so I decided to come home early to spend more time with Mindy. Thanks for dropping her off!"

Eunice-unni smiled. She looked happy that I could spend more time with Dad.

"No problem," she said. "Have fun, Mindy!"

Dad and I waved as she left.

"Okay, Mindy. I have a surprise for you. Close your eyes and take my hand."

It was a weird thing for Dad to ask, but I closed my eyes and grabbed his hand anyway. I trusted him!

Gently, Dad pulled me forward. As we moved, I tried to picture where we were in the house. And I wondered what was going on.

"Okay, open your eyes," Dad said at last.

At first, I was confused. Even though I had

opened my eyes, everything was still dark!

But then I saw them. Five small candles. And below the candles was . . .

"A MINT CHOCOLATE CHIP ICE CREAM CAKE!" I shrieked. "But it's not even my birthday!"

Dad turned the lights back on. He stood there by the table with a grin on his face.

"I know," he said. "But I wanted to congratulate you on making it through your first week at your new school! I was actually planning something for last Friday, but the timing was bad since that's when you got in trouble. So we're celebrating today!"

"Thanks, Dad." I gave him a big hug. "Does this mean I can get a puppy for my birthday?"

Dad looked confused. "Huh?"

"Well, you can't do the surprise candles and ice cream cake again since you already did it now. Doing the same thing twice is boring. The only way to make things *even better* for my birthday is to get me a puppy!"

Dad laughed. "You are a tough customer, Mindy.

Let's settle in a little longer, and we'll see. We can save up some money for one."

It wasn't a yes, but it was better than a no. I still had a chance at the puppy!

Dad cut the ice cream cake into slices and put them onto plates. Two big ones for him and two little ones for me. I ate my ice cream cake so quickly that I almost got a brain freeze.

"Careful!" Dad laughed, his mouth full of ice cream cake. But then he winced. "Ow, brain freeze."

I giggled. "You're so silly, Appa!"

He laughed with me, and soon we were both laughing really loudly.

Maybe things would be okay after all.

Acknowledgments

This book wouldn't have been possible without my life experiences and the many different people I encountered. I moved around a lot as a kid, and at one point, like Mindy, I even moved from California to Florida. I was always "the new kid" and probably wouldn't have made it this far without all the friends I met along the way.

First and foremost, I'd like to thank my parents, who tried their best to raise me in a country that was entirely new to them. Thank you for giving me the varied experiences that would be so vital to my books. 사랑해요.

Second, I would like to thank the teachers I

had while growing up. Not all of my teachers were good, but most of them were amazing and inspired me in so many different ways. Special thanks goes to Ms. Opal Brown, without whom fourth-grade me would have never even written her first book. Thank you also to Ms. Sheila Holsinger, Ms. Ellen Johnston, and Ms. Silvera. I'd also like to include Janet Ohanis in this category, even though she was already retired by the time I met her. Thank you all for dedicating your lives to teaching kids like me and changing countless lives through your wisdom and encouragement.

A writer is a lost, lonely penguin stranded in the middle of Antarctica without her friends, and I'm so glad I didn't have to go on this journey alone. Thank you to Jennifer Cheung, Allyson Smith, Jason Terry, and the other friends I made nearly twenty years ago at Wadsworth Elementary. We had our differences in the very beginning, but overall, thanks to you, my real-life experience as the new girl in Florida was much happier than Mindy's. Thank you also to my friends from different parts of the country: Chelsea Chang, Shiyun Sun, Luke Chou, Bernice Yau, Anita Chen, Brianna Lei, Annie Lee, Kaiti Liu, and Angelica Tran.

I need a whole other section for my writer friends, because you've all helped me in so many different ways. Thank you to Aneeqah Naeem, my number one cheerleader and "unofficial publicist." Our writing dates were literally life changing, and I hope there are many more to come. Thank you also to Francesca Flores, Akemi Dawn Bowman, Katie Zhao, Amelie Zhao, Rebecca Kuang, Suzie Chang, Elly Ha, Andrea Tang, Dahlia Adler, Marieke Nijkamp, Kat Cho, Axie Oh, Nafiza Azad, and the entirety of the #magicsprintingsquad. I love all of you and wish you the best.

Thank you to my courageous and savvy agent, Penny Moore, and my insightful, fellow-lover-of-cute-things editor, Alyson Heller. You both worked tirelessly to bring Mindy into this world, and I appreciate everything you do. You are basically her honorary aunties. Here's to many more happy tears as we continue on this journey together.

Last but not least, thank you to Andrew Su, who believed in me when I didn't believe in myself. Thanks for the countless times you screamed, "OMG SO CUTE!" whenever I sent you excerpts of Mindy's story. I'm not sure I'd have ever gotten the courage to write this book—and made it as cute as I possibly could—without you.

Don't miss Mindy's next adventure!

My name is Mindy Kim.

I'm almost eight years old, or at least, that's how old I am in the United States. In Korea, though, I'm nine! That's what Dad told me as he drove me to school.

"Korean people calculate age differently," he said. "You're already one year old when you're born, and then you get one year older on New Year's Day, instead of getting older on your birthday."

I got really excited, since it's been eight years since I was born. One plus eight is nine, and nine years old was *definitely* old enough to get a puppy. And even better yet, Lunar New Year was this Saturday!

"Does this mean that I'll turn ten this weekend?" I asked, throwing my backpack in the back seat.

Dad laughed. "No, silly. People only age up on the first of January *or* on Lunar New Year, not both."

I sat back into my seat with a big huff. "What's the point of two New Years if you can only age up on one?"

Dad shook his head as he pulled into the school's parking lot. "It's an important part of our culture, Mindy. It goes way back to the times when our ancestors in Korea used the lunar calendar to tell time. Tell you what, why don't we go to the Lunar New Year parade in Orlando this weekend? I saw an ad for it the other day. It looks like it'll be fun!"

Dad smiled at me, but I was unconvinced. The last time Dad said something would be "fun," I ended up watching a boring show about really slow slugs all by myself because he fell asleep in five minutes.

Plus, so much has changed since the last time we celebrated Lunar New Year. Last year, Dad, Mom, and I celebrated with the other Korean people in our neighborhood. We played really fun games like yutnori and jegichagi, ate so many yummy rice cakes, and even sang karaoke! There was no way that we could have as much fun this year as we did then.

Not without Mom.

Now the only other Korean family in our neighborhood is Eunice's, and they were going to Seattle to visit their relatives for the holiday. It was just going to be me and Dad.

"The parade will be fun," Dad said again. "It'll be good for us to leave the house."

I sighed. Dad really wanted to go to the parade! And I didn't want to make him sad by saying I didn't want to go.

"Okay," I said. "I'll go to the parade."

Dad beamed. "Great! See you after school, honey."

"Bye, Appa," I said, using the Korean word for "Daddy."

I headed toward the school, my shoulders slumped. I was not looking forward to Lunar New Year. Not anymore.

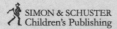